Gunilla Wolde

Betsy's Baby Brother

Random House 🏠 **New York**

First American Edition, 1975

All rights reserved under International and Pan-American Copyright Conventions. Published in the United States by Random House, Inc., New York. Illustrations and original text first published in Sweden as *Emma och Lillebror* by Almqvist & Wiksell Förlag AB, Stockholm. Copyright © 1974 by Gunilla Wolde and Almqvist & Wiksell Förlag AB. ISBN: 0-394-83162-4 (trade ed.) ISBN: 0-394-93162-9 (library ed.) Library of Congress Catalog Card Number: 75-7568

Printed in Great Britain

Betsy has a baby brother.
He is much smaller than Betsy.

He has tiny hands, tiny feet, and
a tiny little nose like a button.

When he is asleep he is very, very quiet.

When he is awake he often cries.
He makes so much noise
you can hear him all over the house.

Sometimes Betsy's baby brother cries
because he is hungry.

Then Mommy holds him in her lap
and feeds him.

Betsy doesn't like it when her mother spends so much time feeding him. She would like to give him away to another lady.

She wishes she could be
a baby all over again.
Then she would have Mommy
all to herself.

After her baby brother finishes eating,
it is time for his bath.

Mommy asks Betsy to get his diapers, soap, and baby ointment. Now Betsy is glad she is not a baby. She can reach the things by herself.

Betsy's brother lies on a blanket
while she changes his diaper.
She takes off his overalls,
and he smiles at her.

Then she takes off his wet diaper.
Her baby brother is still too little
to use the potty.

Now Mommy washes him.
She has to be sure
she gets him very clean.

Before Betsy puts a clean diaper on him,
she spreads ointment on his bottom.
It keeps him from getting red and sore
when he wets his diaper.

Her baby brother wiggles and kicks
while Betsy tries to put on his overalls.

Suddenly he grabs a handful of her hair
and tugs very hard. It hurts.

Mommy explains that babies love to grab at everything with their tiny little fingers.

She gives him some applesauce.
He doesn't like it. He spits it out.
"Maybe he wants
my apple,"
says Betsy.

After Mommy washes his face again,
Betsy's brother begins to yawn and look sleepy.

He lies in his crib, and Betsy talks quietly
to him until he falls asleep.

Betsy thinks that baby brothers are funny.
Sometimes they can be a big nuisance.
But mostly they are cuddly and sweet.